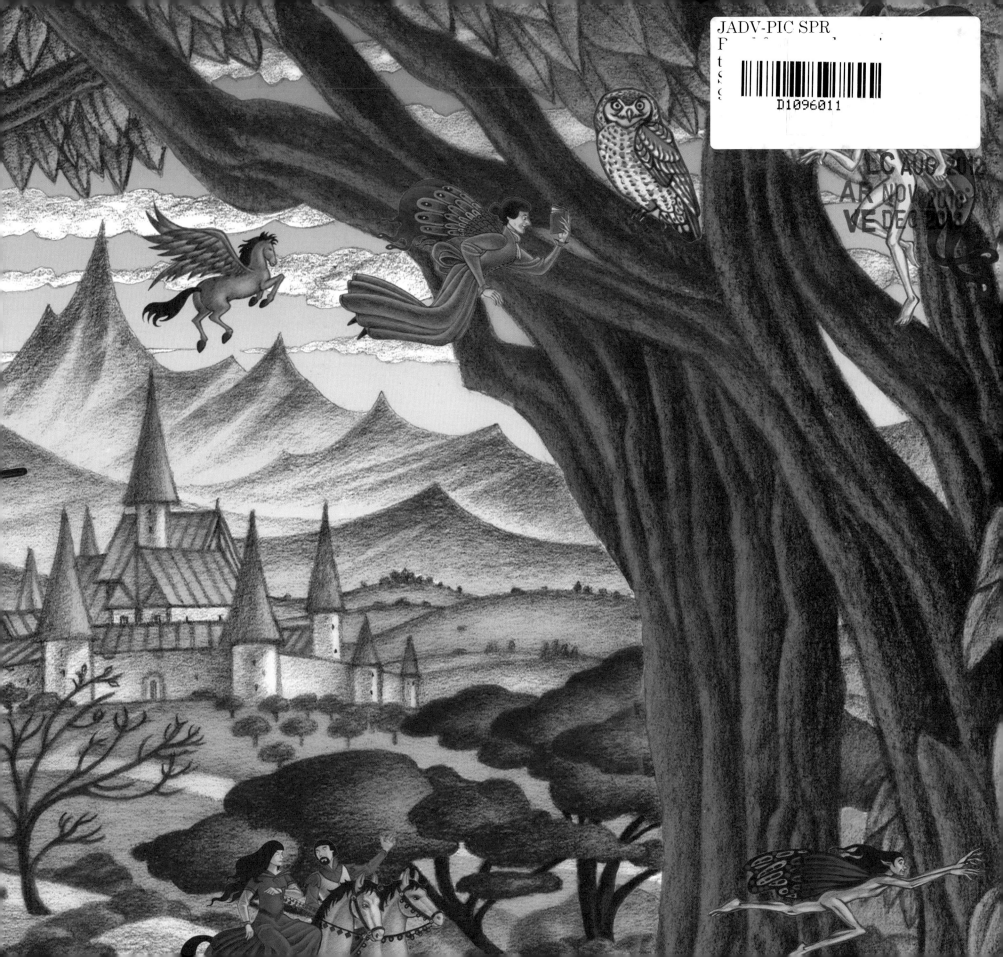

Breakfast on a Dragon's Tail
and other Book Bites

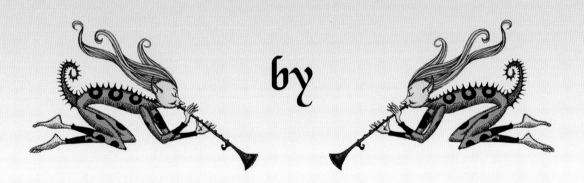

by

Martin Springett

Fitzhenry & Whiteside

Breakfast on a Dragon's Tail
and other Book Bites

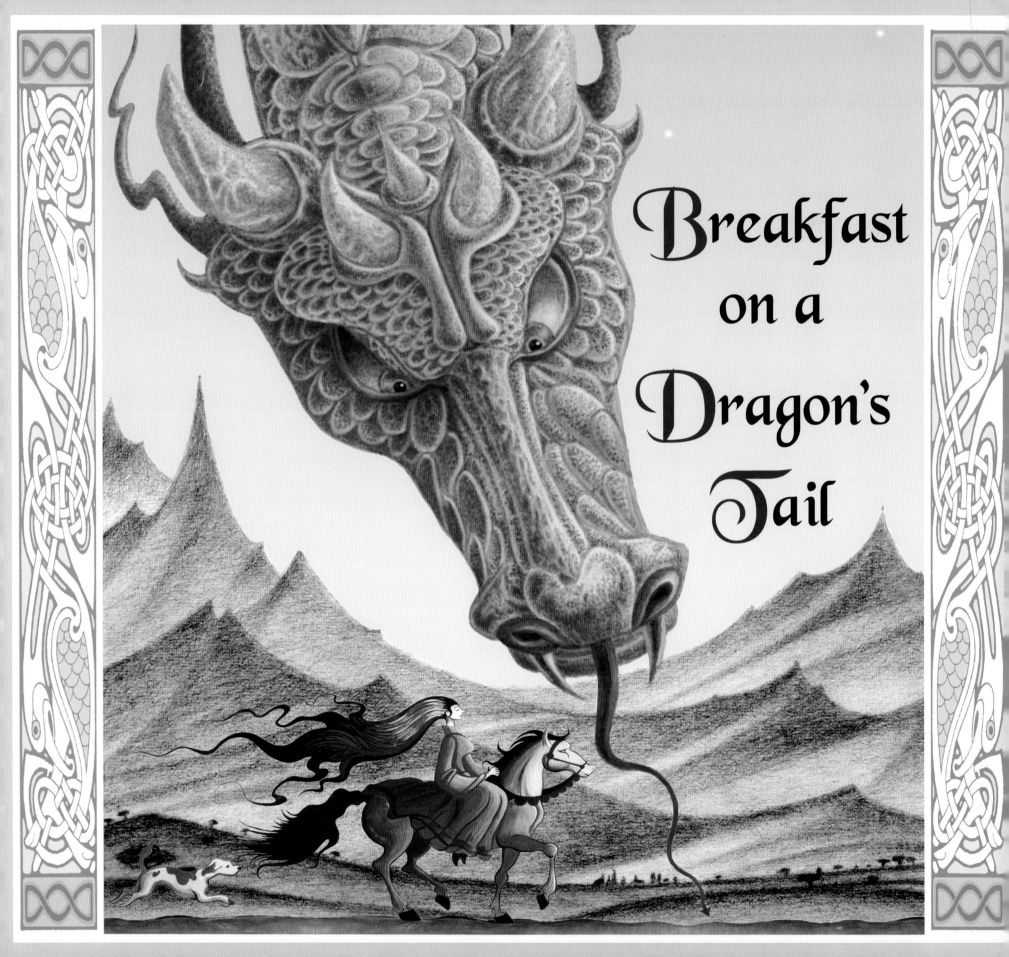

Breakfast
on a
Dragon's
Tail

Breakfast on a Dragon's Tail

One bright summer morning, Princess Miranda decided to go riding. She told her groom, Matthew, to saddle up Thistle, her favourite horse, and call for Pip, her hunting hound.

"I wouldn't go riding today if I were you, my lady," said Matthew. "There be rumours about that Golmogog, the Great Golden Dragon, has returned!"

"Pish posh!" said Miranda. "I don't care about a silly old dragon."

"He may be old, but he isn't silly—and he's big! Why you and that horse of yours could disappear up his left nostril."

"I don't care," said Miranda. "I will have my ride—and no dragon, big or small, is going to stop me!"

(Phew! Either Miranada is very brave or very silly. What do you think happens next?)

Septimus Sneeze & The Ghosts of Gargantua

SEPTIMUS SNEEZE & THE GHOSTS OF GARGANTUA

Septimus Sneeze adored his mother. Septimus Sneeze was convinced that his mother was the most beautiful, most talented mom in the world! The trouble was, Septimus didn't know where in the world she was. An opera singer of great renown, Madame Cecelia Sneeze travelled constantly. After every marvellous performance, it was her habit to visit a desert, jungle, or some other exotic out-of-the-way place and go on what she called, "a little getaway, a little explore."

Her last message to Septimus and his dad was, "See you soon, boys. Don't worry—gone to Gargantua!"

Septimus had tried to find Gargantua on the big map that hung in his mom's rehearsal room, but it was nowhere to be found and it had been a month now since any word had come from his adored mom. Septimus knew he had to go on an "explore" of his own to find Gargantua and his mother!

Colin, his dachshund, was not keen on this idea and hid under the couch for three days. Septimus's dad was even less keen. "I'm an accountant, not an explorer! Your mother will turn up. She always does."

"But Dad, we have to find Mom! We just *have* to!" said Septimus.

"All right Sep, but what do you suggest?" said his dad.

"*Grrrrrowl*," said Colin.

(Gosh! Where in golly is Gargantua, and how will Septimus, Colin, and his dad find Madame Cecelia Sneeze, the opera star?)

The Gloomy Spong
& the Sparkly Girl

The Gloomy Spong & the Sparkly Girl

Once, a long time ago, there lived the Gloomy Spong. The Spong sat and wondered—he wondered (mainly) what he should do next. He shifted this way; he shifted that way. He scratched his bushy eyebrows. He picked at his enormous claws. He licked his spiny tail. He ate a passing fly.

"Something must be done!" he roared. "I know, I shall ask the Harumpf. He is wise and knows all."

The Gloomy Spong spread his leathery wings. He found the Harumpf sitting in a thorn bush eating thimble fruit. "What can be done?" cried the Spong.

"*Harumpf*!" said the Harumpf. "Why ask me? I'm stuck in a thorn bush and very busy. May I suggest a chat with the Egg?"

"I have never found my chats with the Egg to be very satisfying—a bit one-sided."

"That is because you have never asked the *right* question," said the Harumpf.

With a slow, mournful flap and snap, the Gloomy Spong took flight once more. He found the Egg in its usual spot (it didn't get about much). The Gloomy Spong sat atop the Egg for some time and thought hard about his first question. But before he could ask the question, a girl in a sparkly dress wandered out of the forest. She twirled around once, pulled out a wand from her sparkly dress, and tapped the egg lightly. The egg jiggled.

"Who are you?" cried the Spong.

(Who is this Sparkly Girl? Will the Spong get an answer to his important question? What *is* the right question? And what do you think is happening to the Egg?)

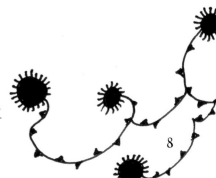

Saffron & Licorice

Every Sunday night, Saffron would have the same dream. She found herself walking down a long road with her dog, Licorice. Way at the end of the road, she saw her school. As she walked closer, she could see what looked like huge statues in front of the imposing building.

At this point in the dream, she wanted to run away, to be anywhere but here, because she knew who these statues were: bullies and teasers—kids who enjoyed making her cry. But somehow she could not turn away. She had to face them, just as she did every day at her school.

She did her best not to look at them as she walked by. Licorice, her best friend, always licked her hand to give her the courage she needed. The really frightening part of the dream was when the statues started to talk; first they made a grumbling, stony sort of sound, like gravel flowing down a metal chute. Then they began to shout and Saffron could make out words—words that were meant to wound.

Usually, these scary sounds would cause Saffron to wake up in a cold sweat. But this time, things suddenly changed.

For the first time in this recurring dream, Licorice barked at the statues. Startled, Saffron somehow found the courage to yell at the looming figures, "I'm not listening to you anymore! I'm not listening!"

Then the statues started to move and as they did so, large cracks appeared in their bodies and faces. Huge chunks fell off them as they moved menacingly towards Saffron and Licorice.

(How will Saffron tackle her bully dilemma in her dream? And will she ever be able confront the real bullies in school?)

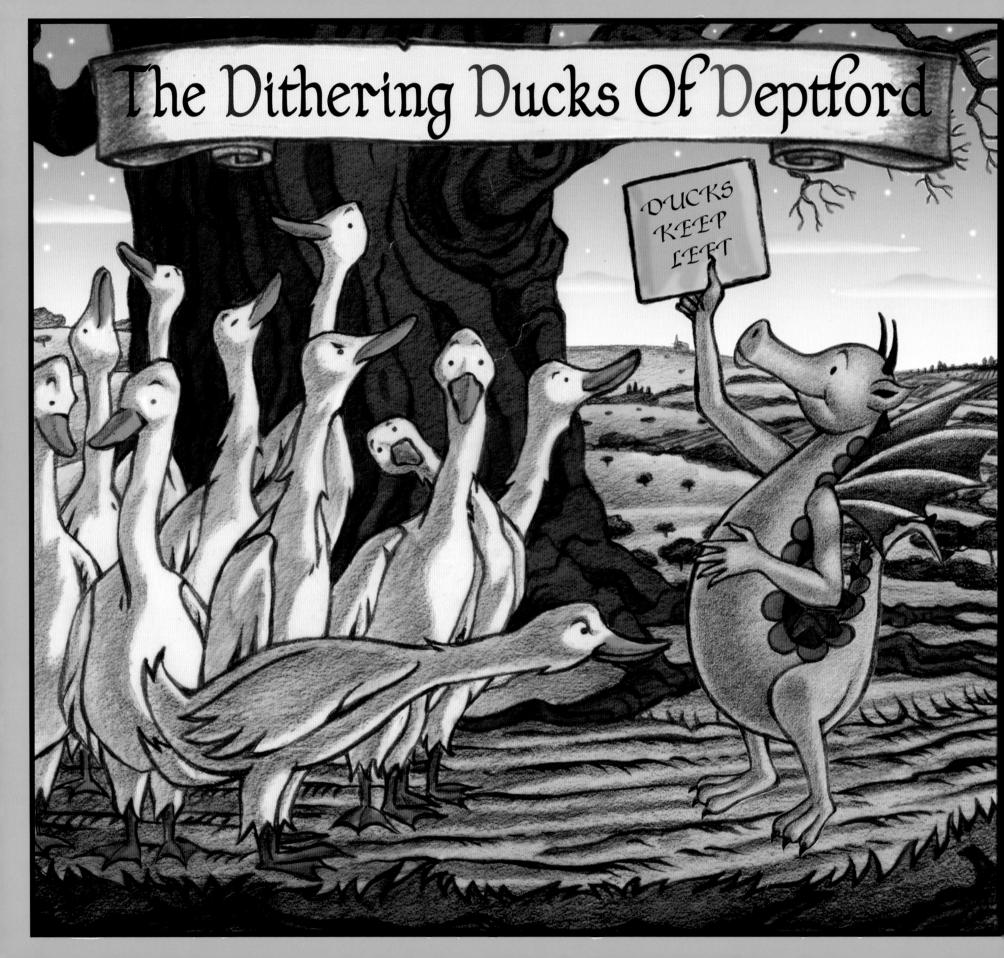

The Dithering Ducks of Deptford

"Are we there yet? Are we there?"

"I recognise this tree—we passed it an hour ago."

"This is not Deptford. This is most *definitely* not Deptford."

"Never listen to a gnome! They are born naughty!"

"That cat was crafty too. Did you see the gleam in its eye? I think it had it in for us."

"Oh no! A *dragon*—that's all we need!"

"Dragons eat ducks. I am certain of it!"

"Well, I'm not taking directions from a dragon, even if he is cute."

"What's he holding up—a sign?"

"Oh, he's one of those *clever* dragons. He expects us to *read*."

"Maybe he's showing off."

"I think it's a book—he's written a book!"

"Never trust a clever dragon, especially one who's written a book!"

"*I* could write a book."

"Well, *I* wouldn't read it. You and your 'Here's a nice gnome. He'll know the way.'"

"Oh, and I suppose your 'Cats are clever, let's ask him!' worked out any better?"

"We must stop dithering and ask this dragon if he knows the way to Deptford."

"I think we are okay. This is a *fruit-eating* dragon, and I happen to know that *fruit-eating* dragons are friendly."

"Oh, really?"

(Will this lot *ever* stop talking? Will the dragon help them get home to Deptford?)

The Nattering Tree

The Nattering Tree was an unusually talkative sort of tree. People would come from many miles around just to sit under the Tree and listen to it natter.

Mostly it spoke to itself: "It's a lovely day... My leaves are gorgeous this year... I could do with more rain... I sometimes wish I was part of a forest..."

Folks had tried talking to the Tree over the years, but it rarely answered anyone. The last time was twenty-five years ago, when a small boy asked a question. Then, all the Tree had said was, "I don't *think* so!"

And it hadn't replied directly to anyone since.

But now, the man who was once that little boy had returned with the same question—and some big earth-moving equipment. Once again, the Tree said, "I don't *think* so!" to his repeated question. It shook its leaves in anger and the ground shuddered.

"Well, that's too bad," said the man as he bent down to pick up a chainsaw.

"You can't cut down the Nattering Tree!" said two little girls who had been sitting contentedly amongst the roots of the Tree, listening to it burble away.

"Oh, but I can," said the man. "I own all this land—including the Tree."

"But this is the Nattering Tree," said one little girl. "You can't do this, you just *can't*!"

(What was the question that the boy asked the Tree? Will the man chop it down?)

ICICLE FINGERS

Once again, Icicle Fingers, the Winter Imp, had woken up and gone off to play in the fields and forests at the wrong time of year. Odd, frozen moments were going on—in the middle of summer! The King and Queen of Winter were outraged.

"Fingers must be taught a lesson," grumbled the King. "He can't just wake up and toddle off when he wants to. He's a Winter Imp, not a Summer Imp!"

"I agree," said the Queen. "This has got to stop. These summer wake-ups are giving me a royal headache!"

"What do you suggest?" asked the King.

"First, let's pop Fingers into a deep-freeze spell for the rest of the summer and fall; then we'll wake him up on the first day of winter and send him on a quest."

"Splendid!" exclaimed the King. "What did you have in mind?"

"The first part will be to discover the true meaning of the winter season," the Queen answered.

"And what would that be?" asked the King.

"I have no idea," laughed the Queen in her flute-like voice.

"Brilliant!" said the King. "And the other part of the quest?"

"To teach the true meaning of winter to the incorrigible Edward Fitchpuddle, the scourge of Fiddlehead Elementary, along the way!"

"We should have done this many winters ago," chuckled the King. "These tasks ought to keep both Icicle Fingers and Edward out of trouble for a good long time!"

(Will Icicle Fingers discover the true meaning of winter? And will he be able to deal with Edward Fitchpuddle, every teacher's nightmare?)

DRACULA AND SON

"Wake up, son! It's time to terrify the neighbourhood!" Papa Drac stretched and yawned, flexing his long, white hands and testing his bright, white fangs with a handy fork. *Ping*! They were solid and scary—ready for all the terrifying stuff he had planned for the surrounding countryside, the lonely farmhouses, and the craggy castles.

"Nah, I'm tired," said Drac Junior. "I wanna sleep in."

"You've already slept in for nine months! It's Hallowe'en —time to sharpen those pearly whites and to practise blood-curdling screeches, climbing down walls, and flapping about in a creepy way!"

"You go ahead, Papa. Wake me up in another three months," said Drac Junior.

"Come on! You know I can't do it without you—we're a team! I need your help tonight. Prince Mustard is out there!"

Junior looked horrified. "The Mustard?" he said. "I don't relish that!"

(Wow! Prince Mustard! Sounds like these guys are in for a hot and frightful night themselves—will they find themselves in a pickle?)

THE TWELVE DANCING CROCODILES

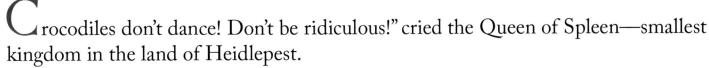

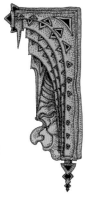

"Crocodiles don't dance! Don't be ridiculous!" cried the Queen of Spleen—smallest kingdom in the land of Heidlepest.

"But your highness," replied her tall and eccentric courtier, Eric the Ever Ready, "there have been sightings deep in the forest of Heem. Twelve young crocodiles a-leaping and cavorting, performing what our loyal knight, Sir Noodlebut the Brave, could only describe as—a dance!"

The great hall fell silent as all eyes turned expectantly to the queen. "What can it mean, Eric?" said the queen. "Are they planning an entertainment, or are they part of a cunning plan to take over the castle after we are lured into amazement at the sight of twelve crocodiles prancing about?"

"They are, according to our witness, very small crocodiles your Highness, and..."

"Yes, Eric, there is something else?"

"They are, um, *cute*."

The queen stood up and paced nervously in front of her throne. "And they seek our permission to perform here, in the Great Hall?"

"Indeed they do, your Majesty," said Eric. "The boy Tillman delivered the note yesterday."

The queen stopped pacing and stared at Eric. "Tillman, the Magician's son?" A murmur ran through the crowded hall. "Tillman, who vanished along with the Twelve Dancing Princesses?"

Eric's bushy eyebrows performed their own eccentric dance. "The same, your Majesty, the same!"

The queen returned to her throne, sat down with a thump, and said very quietly, "Bring the boy here, now!"

A guard called out, "Find the boy Tillman! Bring him to court!"

And then another. "The boy Tillman. Bring him to court!" The command echoed throughout the castle.

(What does the boy Tillman know? What—or who—are these twelve unusually talented crocodiles?)

The Who That is Me

$\mathcal{M}$iriam always liked to share her Sunday afternoon snack with Mog, her dog, in a forest glade, just behind her parents' farm house. Afterward, Mog usually spent some time amongst the trees, but today she came back very quickly and sat panting beside Miriam.

"What is it, Mog?" said Miriam. She could tell that Mog had that expectant look about her, as though she was waiting for something.

Soon, Miriam heard a huffling, puffling sort of sound, a crackling of twigs, a *disturblement* of leaves. Then something very large and green wandered into view.

Mog gave a little woof and a little whine.

"Who are you?" asked Miriam in a high voice.

"Precisely, precisely! You'll do very nicely!" said the big, green thing.

"What are you?" said Miriam.

"Everyone is a Which, a What, or a Why, but if you don't house a Who, he'll most certainly cry." And here a big blue tear rolled down the very long nose of the green stranger.

"You are a Who?" asked Miriam.

"That is me," said the big, green galoot. He shook himself, sending clouds of brown dust into the air.

Mog's big, black nose started twitching madly, catching the new Who smell. But instead of barking at the Who, she wagged her tail and laid her head down on his big, green, furry paw.

"Well," declared Miriam, "if Mog likes you, that's good enough for me."

"Precisely, precisely!" repeated the Who, with a smile. "You'll *both* do very nicely. I hope it's not long before I belong!"

(What will Miriam do with the big, green guy, and is there room
on the family farm for a homeless Who?)

22

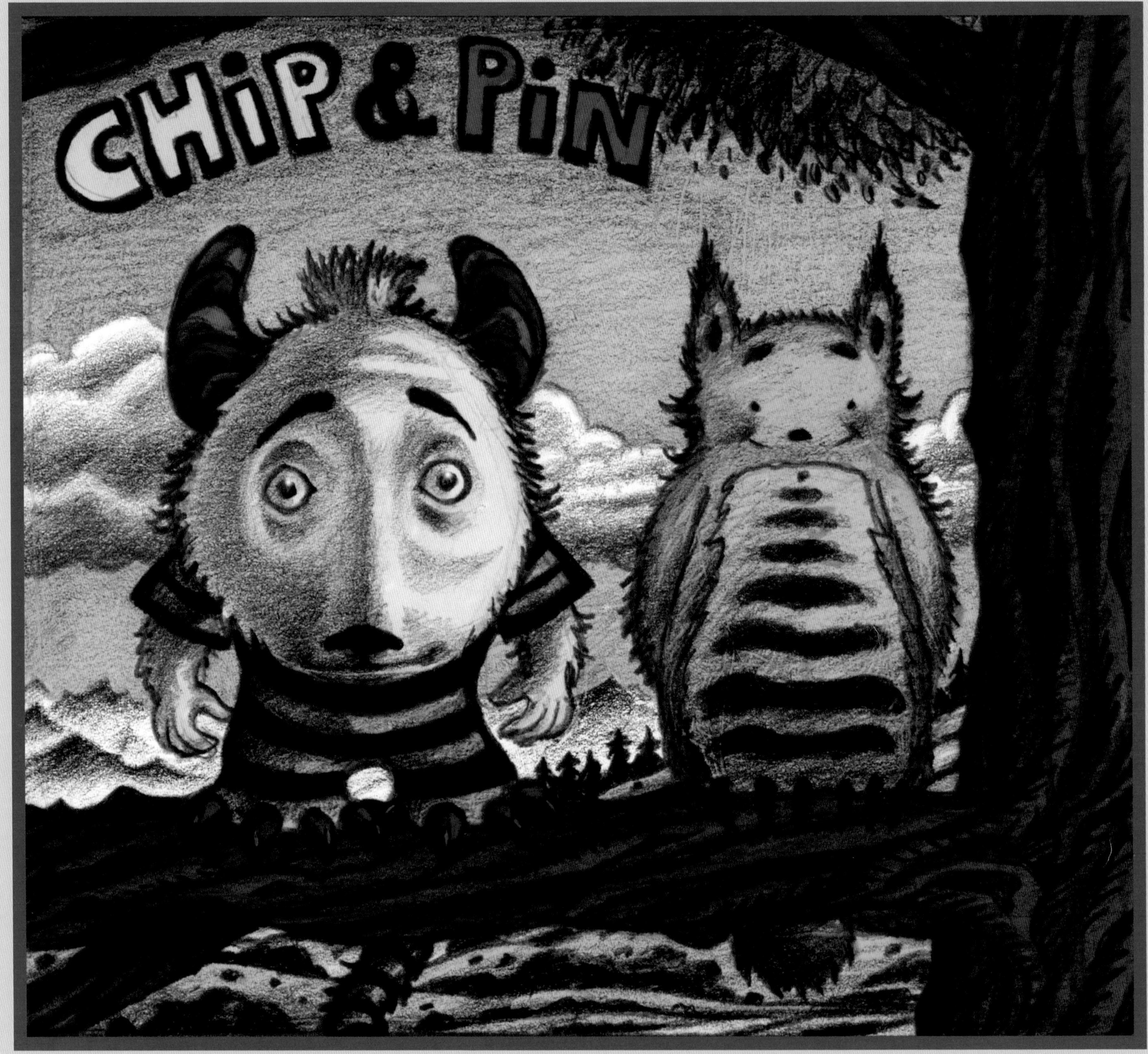
CHiP & PiN

CHIP AND PIN

High in the mountains of the Pacific Northwest, two old friends sat talking.

"It's a beautiful day, Chip," said Pin.

"That may be so, but I see clouds on the horizon—great, billowy, dark things that suggest a storm is moving in," sighed Chip.

"Well, live in the moment, Chip," said Pin. "It's sunny and warm right now."

"That may be so," grumbled Chip, "but soon night will fall, and it will be damp and cold."

"We will have a full moon tonight, Chip! The mountains will look beautiful in the soft, silver moonlight," said Pin.

"That may be so, Pin," harrumphed Chip, "but we may be in danger from the great Awk that hunts by the bright light of the moon and enjoys eating small, furry critters like us."

"Well," said Pin, "that could be *awk*-erward." Pin began to vibrate with silent laughter.

"WHAT?" yelled Chip.

(*Phew*! How does Pin get through the day with a friend like Chip? They must have something in common. What do you think happens next?)

24

GLIMMERLAND

GLIMMERLAND

Annie lived with her grandparents in a big, gloomy house in the country, far away from any of her school friends. Because she rarely had any visitors, she was used to being alone and had grown accustomed to amusing herself with her main interests: reading and music.

Annie's favourite book was an odd little volume full of colourful pictures called *The Glimms*. It was about a strange, faraway land where everything was musical, eccentric, bright, and full of adventures.

"It's an old book, but a good one," said her kindly Grandpa Ted when he gave it to her. "I think you'll enjoy it."

Annie found herself dreaming about Glimmerland. "I'd love to go there," she thought after she had read and re-read the story several times.

One rainy afternoon, after noodling on the piano keys in a half-hearted way, she decided to look through the huge pile of old sheet music in the piano bench. She was surprised to find a piece of music called *Glimmerland.* Excitedly, she propped the music up on the piano and began to play...

As the music unfurled beneath her fingers, much to her amazement the left side of the old upright piano popped open like a door. Cautiously, she peered inside the piano and saw a short flight of steps. Of course, she had to investigate!

At the bottom of the stairs was a small door with strange squiggles and designs surrounding it. Best of all, sitting in front of the door, beaming broadly was—a *Glimm*. He beckoned to her and pushed open the door...

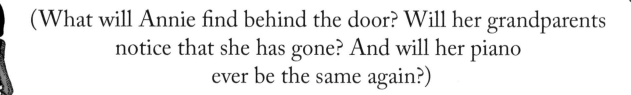

(What will Annie find behind the door? Will her grandparents notice that she has gone? And will her piano ever be the same again?)

THE BOOK OF WONDERING

THE BOOK OF WONDERING

Whenever John picked up the *Book of Wondering* and began to read, he saw things—things just out the corner of his eye. Fleeting fairy shapes, birds and dragons, and once, a noble lion. His sister Gracie didn't believe him. She didn't see what John saw, although she loved the story just as much as he did.

She did see their dog Django, though, who dashed toward them and ran about barking madly whenever John started reading.

"You see?" said John, "Django can see them, too."

Gracie rolled her eyes.

"John," she said, "it's a lovely story, but it's *not* real."

One Sunday afternoon, as John began to read the book to Gracie, they could hear the sound of barking in the back field.

"There you are," laughed John. "Even from a distance, old Django can sense there are strange things around whenever I read this book."

"John," said Gracie, "that's *not* Django."

They both listened intently to the next sound...a low, rumbly sort of sound.

"That sounds like..."

"*A lion!*" said John.

(Is this a friendly Story Book Lion, or something a little more dangerous? What else will John and Gracie see?)

Author's Note

The most important part of creating a story is your imagination. The next important part is how you organise the story so that your readers will enjoy the tale you have created.

Simply put, your story should have a beginning, a middle, and an end. I have started the story for you, and now it's up to you to create the next two parts. How will it all turn out in the end? That's what makes all of us turn the pages of a story while reading, isn't it, whether it's a chapter book, picture book, or graphic novel; what is going to happen next?

You can finish the story in whatever way you wish.
- a comic or graphic novel
- a picture book
- a poem
- a mural
- a film
- a chapter book
- a song
- out loud (in the oral folk tradition of the many different cultures around the world)
- even a chalk drawing on the sidewalk!

However you do it, make sure you finish the tale—after breakfast, of course!

Here are some things to keep in mind when you are finishing your story:

⭐ Who are my main characters and how are they likely to behave? What are they likely to do or say?

⭐ Does the action lead up to a climax (the most exciting or important part of the story)?

⭐ Is there a problem that the character(s) solve in the end?

All of these beginnings will lead you on a path of discovery, and that's what makes story-telling so much fun.

Share Your Stories!

Please visit www.fitzhenry.ca/breakfastbites if you would like to send us your finished stories or read what other kids have written. Teachers and parents will also find useful information and classroom activities there.

I look forward to reading these tales very much.

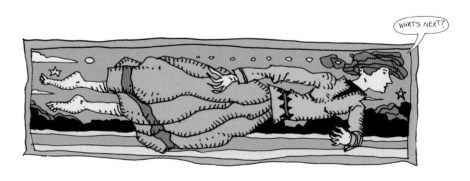

Martin Springett

This book is for all the dedicated teachers and librarians I have met in my literary travels across Canada in the last twenty years. —M.S.

Text and illustrations copyright © 2011 Martin Springett

Published in Canada by Fitzhenry & Whiteside, 195 Allstate Parkway, Markham, Ontario L3R 4T8

Published in the United States by Fitzhenry & Whiteside, 311 Washington Street, Brighton, Massachusetts 02135

www.fitzhenry.ca   godwit@fitzhenry.ca

10 9 8 7 6 5 4 3 2 1

Library and Archives Canada Cataloguing in Publication
Springett, Martin
Breakfast on a dragon's tail / Martin Springett.
ISBN 978-155455-193-4
Complete data avaliable on file with Library and Archives Canada

Publisher Cataloging-in-Publication Data (U.S)
Springett, Martin.
Breakfast on a Dragon's Tail / Martin Springett.
[32] p. : col. ill. ; 28 x 25 cm.
Summary: An interactive collection of illustrated book covers for thirteen different storybooks along with the beginning, but the reader writes the ending.
ISBN: 978-155455-193-4
Complete data available on file with Library of Congress

Fitzhenry & Whiteside acknowledges with thanks the Canada Council for the Arts, and the Ontario Arts Council for their support of our publishing program. We acknowledge the financial support of the Government of Canada through the Canada Book Fund (CBF) for our publishing activities.

Canada Council for the Arts **Conseil des Arts du Canada**

ONTARIO ARTS COUNCIL CONSEIL DES ARTS DE L'ONTARIO

Cover and interior design by Martin Springett & Daniel Choi
Printed and Bound in Hong Kong, China by Paramount Printing Ltd., July 2011, job# 132151